LITTLE TOBY
and the
BIG HAIR

KIM AND EUGENIE FERNANDES

FIREFLY BOOKS

A FIREFLY BOOK

Cataloging in Publication Data

Fernandes, Eugenie, 1943-
    Little Toby and the big hair

ISBN 1-55209-273-9 (bound)   ISBN 1-55209-257-7 (pbk.)

I. Fernandes, Kim. II. Title.

PS8561.E75965L5 1998   jC813'.54   C98-930890-1
PZ7.F47Li 1998

Design by Avril Orloff

Published in the United States in 1998
by Firefly Books (U.S.) Inc.
P.O. Box 1338, Ellicott Station
Buffalo, New York, USA
14205

To Pop, who doesn't have much hair. — E.F.
To Robyn, who doesn't have much hair…yet. — K.F.

Printed and bound in Canada

"I don't want to cut my hair,"
said Toby.
"I'm going to let it grow!"

She let it grow all the way
down to her knees.
It was curly, and twisty,
and bouncy, and BIG.
Some of the children teased her.
Some of the grown-ups were alarmed.
But her friends liked her
any way at all.

Puppies snuggled in her neck
and hid underneath her hair.
Little goats nibbled it.
Robins built a nest with it.
Sometimes candies got stuck in her hair.
Sometimes her hair got tangled in the trees.
But Toby didn't care.
She liked having long hair.

Mother said, "Long hair is too much trouble.
It's always falling in your face —
sometimes you can't even see where you're going."
This was true.

One day Toby rolled right into the duck pond.
There was a gigantic splash.
Ducks and fish and feathers
went flying in all directions.

Mother went racing into the water.
"Are you alright?" she cried.
Toby wasn't hurt, but her hair
was all tangled up with turtles,
and frogs, and crawdads and lily pads.

"You look like a mermaid," said Mother.
Then she carefully untangled all the creatures.
Pretty soon the mermaid looked just like Toby.

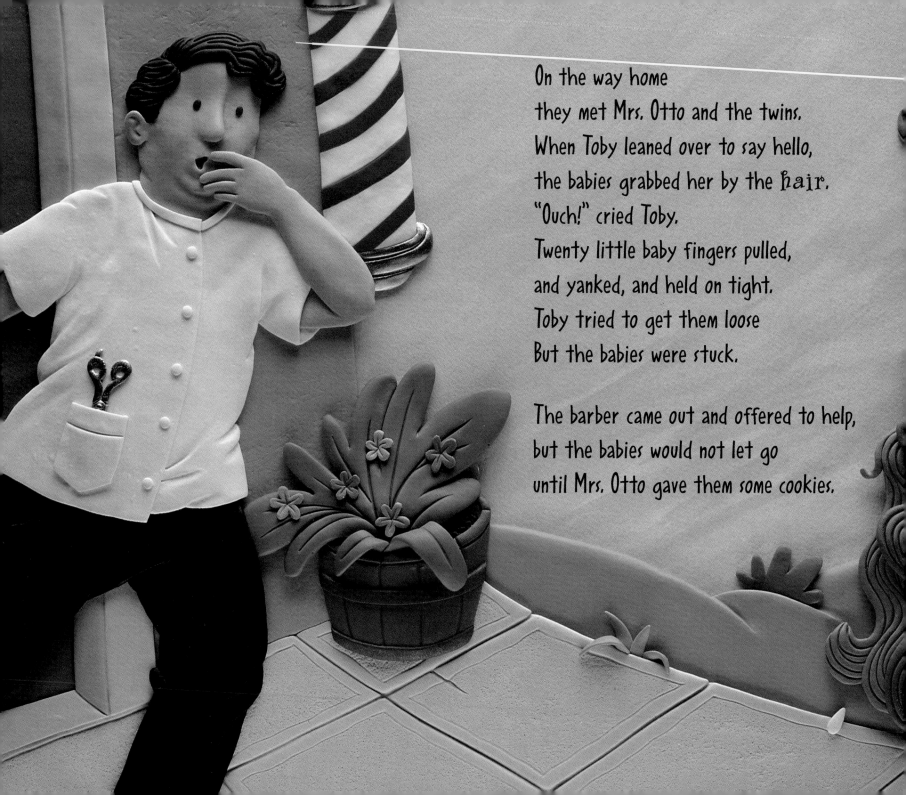

On the way home
they met Mrs. Otto and the twins.
When Toby leaned over to say hello,
the babies grabbed her by the hair.
"Ouch!" cried Toby.
Twenty little baby fingers pulled,
and yanked, and held on tight.
Toby tried to get them loose
But the babies were stuck.

The barber came out and offered to help,
but the babies would not let go
until Mrs. Otto gave them some cookies.

"Little Toby," said the barber,
"your hair is so BIG.
Let me cut it nice and short."
"It will look pretty that way,"
added Mother hopefully.
But Toby shook her head.
"No thank you, Mr. Barber.
I'm going to let my hair grow forever.
Someday I will have the longest hair
in the whole world."
"Oh my!" exclaimed the barber.
"Won't that be awfully heavy?"

"It *will* be heavy," said Toby,
"but I will have one zebra, two camels,
three leopards and a cow,
two toucans, four chickens,
one hippo and a mouse
just to carry my hair.
They will follow me everywhere."
The barber was amazed.

"Please Toby," said Mother,
"let's cut your hair.
You don't need long hair in the summer.
It's too hot."
"But I need long hair in the winter,"
said Toby. "It keeps me warm.
In fact, it keeps me so warm
that I can go sledding in my bathing suit,
and flowers will bloom all around me in the snow."

After that crazy hair day,
Mother tried to ignore Toby's tangles.

Then one day, as they were
getting ready for the family picnic,
Toby's hair kept falling in the food.
Mother finally had a fit.
"That's it!" she cried. "No more hair!"

Toby jumped and scared the cat.
The cat jumped and bumped the flour.
The flour went flying through the air,
spilling all over Toby's hair.

Toby went racing outside into the yard.
Flour flying, arms thrashing, hair flapping.
It was frightful!
Mrs. Pickett was terrified.
In a panic she called the dogcatcher.
"Hurry! There's a wild creature
in the neighbor's yard."

Before the dogcatcher got there,
Grandfather arrived.
"Stand back!" shrieked Mrs. Pickett.
"That creature is ferocious!!"
Grandfather took one look and said,
"Don't worry, Mrs. Pickett,
this creature is my granddaughter."

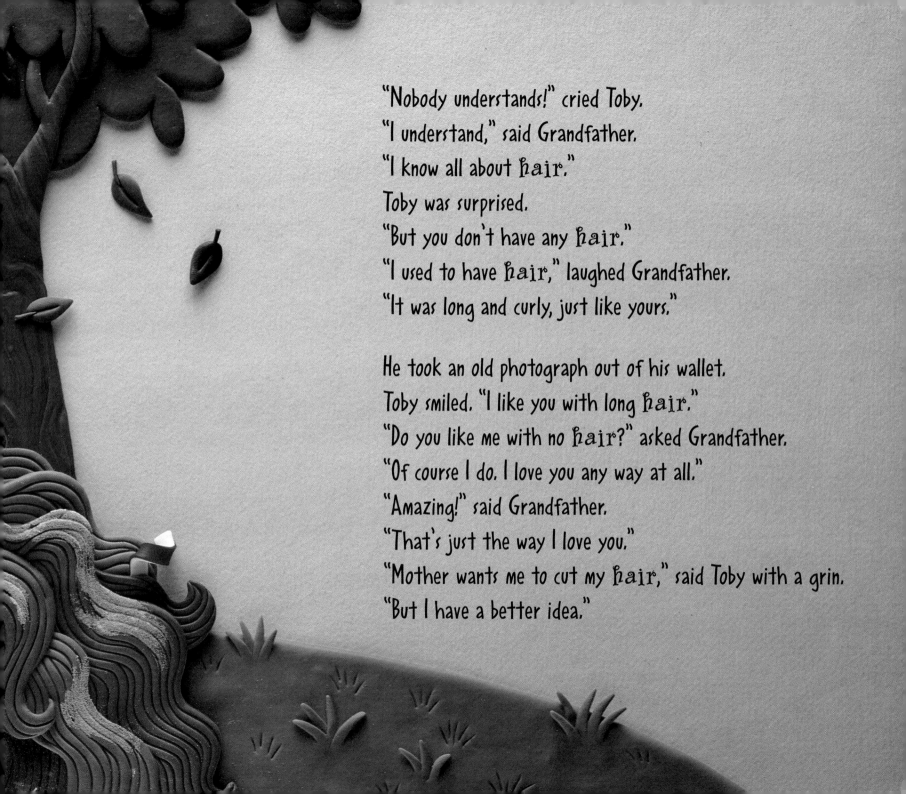

"Nobody understands!" cried Toby.

"I understand," said Grandfather.

"I know all about hair."

Toby was surprised.

"But you don't have any hair."

"I used to have hair," laughed Grandfather.

"It was long and curly, just like yours."

He took an old photograph out of his wallet.

Toby smiled. "I like you with long hair."

"Do you like me with no hair?" asked Grandfather.

"Of course I do. I love you any way at all."

"Amazing!" said Grandfather.

"That's just the way I love you."

"Mother wants me to cut my hair," said Toby with a grin.

"But I have a better idea."

Toby and Grandfather went inside.

They washed all the flour out of Toby's hair.

Bubbles filled the bathroom

and floated out the window.

Grandfather rinsed away the bubbles

and brushed away the tangles.

They dried Toby's hair.

They braided it and ribboned it.

"There," said Toby,

"it's beautiful this way too."

By the time they went downstairs,
the family picnic had begun.
"Toby," said Aunt Monica,
"your hair looks so pretty today!"

Mother hugged her.
Father was pleased.
Everyone laughed and ate
and had a wonderful time —
even Toby.

When the picnic was over,
Mother and Toby went for a walk.
By now, Toby's hair had begun to hurt,
so they untied the ribbons
and took out the braids.
Toby's hair tumbled happily in all directions.

"Ribbons are perfect for parties," said Mother,
"but your hair is beautiful this way too."

As they walked along together,
starlight got tangled in Toby's hair.